This edition published by Parragon Books Ltd in 2015 and distributed by

Parragon Inc.
440 Park Avenue South, 13th Floor
New York, NY 10016
www.parragon.com

Polar Bear Boy: Text © Gillian Shields, Illustrations © Dubravka Kolanovic. First published 2012 by Gullane Children's Books. Little Rabbit Waits for the Moon: Text © Beth Shoshan, Illustrations © Stephanie Peel. First published 2004 by Meadowside Children's Books. If Big Can ... I Can: Text © Beth Shoshan, Illustrations © Petra Brown. First published 2006 by Meadowside Children's Books. The Adventures of the Owl and the Pussycat: Text © Coral Rumble, Illustrations © Charlotte Cooke. First published 2013 by Parragon Books Ltd by arrangement with Meadowside Children's Books. If You Can ... We Can: Text © Beth Shoshan, Illustrations © Petra Brown. First published 2008 by Meadowside Children's Books. Hernando Fandango: Text and Illustrations © Rachel Swirles. First published 2013 by Meadowside Children's Books. I Love You, Alfie Cub: Text © Angela McAllister, Illustration © Daniel Howarth. First published 2013 by Parragon Books Ltd by arrangement with Gullane Children's Books.

Published by arrangement with Meadowside Children's Books and Gullane Children's Books
185 Fleet Street, London, EC4A 2HS

ISBN 978-1-4748-3307-3

Printed in China

Read to Me,
Mommy

7 delightful stories
for bedtime reading

PaRragon

Bath · New York · Singapore · Hong Kong · Cologne · Delhi
Melbourne · Amsterdam · Johannesburg · Auckland · Shenzhen

Contents

Polar Bear Boy   8
Written by Gillian Shields
Illustrated by Dubravka Kolanovic

For Jamie Graham, who introduced me to polar bears—G. S.
To Philip Begonja, who could see all the mountains,
the sea, and the stars—D. K.

Little Rabbit Waits for the Moon   28
Written by Beth Shoshan
Illustrated by Stephanie Peel

For Steph—B. S.
For Carla, Marshall, and Liam—S. P.

If Big Can ... I Can   48
Written by Beth Shoshan
Illustrated by Petra Brown

For Danny, Beth, Mimi, and Joseph—B. S.
For Callum, and Iain—P. B.

**The Adventures of the Owl
and the Pussycat**   74
Written by Coral Rumble
Illustrated by Charlotte Cooke

For Andy, the BUMP, and Amelia—my very own naughty seagull—C. C.
For Jean and Gordon (my parents)—C. R.

If You Can ... We Can   96

Written by Beth Shoshan
Illustrated by Petra Brown

For you, me, and all of us!—B. S.
For Lewis and Samantha—P. B

Hernando Fandango   118

Written and illustrated
by Rachel Swirles

For Lizzie, who's been with me all the way—R. S.

I Love You, Alfie Cub!   140

Written by Angela McAllister
Illustrated by Daniel Howarth

To Paula, Tim, Samuel, Emily,
and George—A. McA.
To Paula, my advocate, my mentor,
my friend—thank you!—D. H.

Polar Bear Boy

It was dark at bedtime.
Outside there were black shadows on the snow.

"Dad," whispered Jamie. "Polar Bear is scared!"
"Scared of what?" asked Dad.
"The shadows," said Jamie. "And the night noises. And . . .

"DRAGONS!"

"Hmm," said Dad, "that's strange. Because when
I was your age, my father told me that
polar bears aren't scared of anything."

"Not even the dark?" asked Jamie.

"No," smiled Dad.

"And neither are polar bear boys."

10

"Am I a polar bear boy?" said Jamie.

"Well," said Dad. "You might be . . .

11

"Do you remember, one very dark night,
your polar bear woke up ready for an adventure ..."
"Tell me about it!" said Jamie.
"He stretched and licked his paws,
and breathed his warm bear breath.

His breath became a breeze,
then a wind ...

12

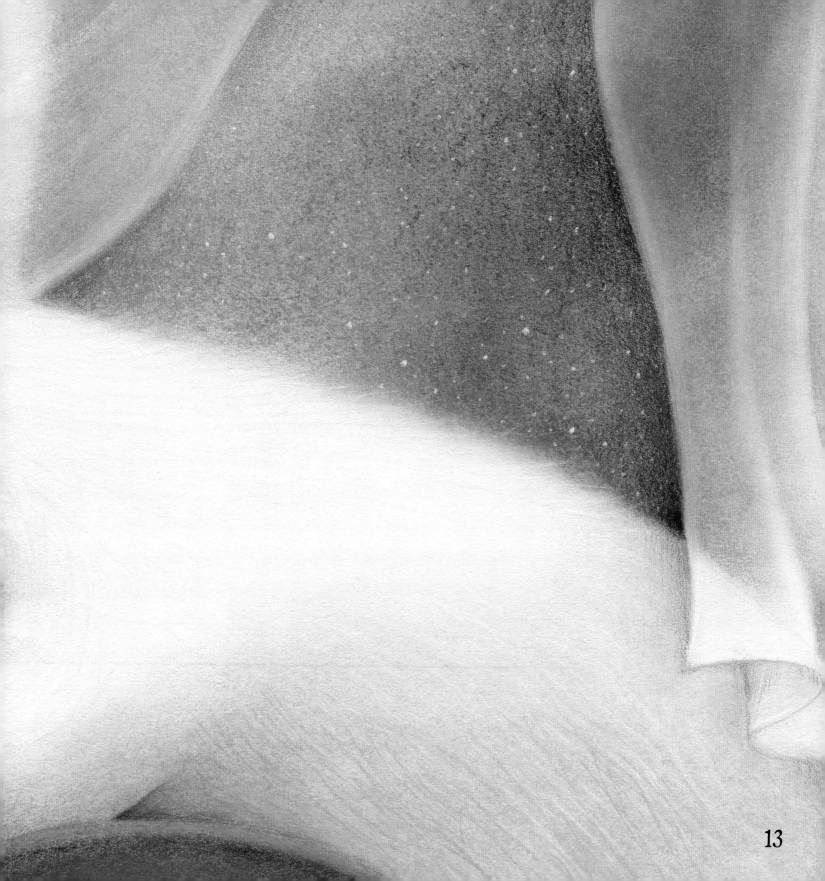

"It blew you out of the garden and over the fields.
The night was soft and beautiful.
In the distance, the sea was sparkling under the stars."

"Did we see any mermaids?" asked Jamie.

14

15

"Of course!" laughed Dad.
"They were sitting on the rocks, singing about treasure.
So you went to look for it in the caves."

"Were the caves very dark?"
asked Jamie, looking
a little worried.
"As dark as midnight,"
said Dad . . .

"But Polar Bear led the way,
as brave as brave."

17

"Wait!" cried Jamie. "There was a dragon
in the cave, guarding the treasure!"
"Polar Bear roared and chased it away,"
said Dad. "He wasn't scared."

Jamie smiled. "I'd forgotten that.
It was a silly dragon, wasn't it?"
"Very silly," laughed Dad.

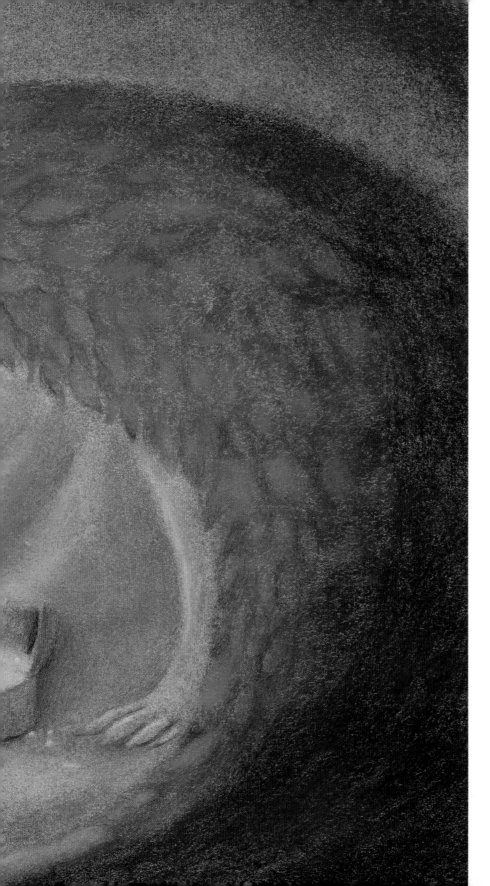

"Then we looked at all the treasure," said Jamie. "Rubies and pearls and big lumps of gold!"

"Wow!" said Dad. "And what happened next?"

"I left the treasure for the mermaids," said Jamie. "Then we flew away!"

19

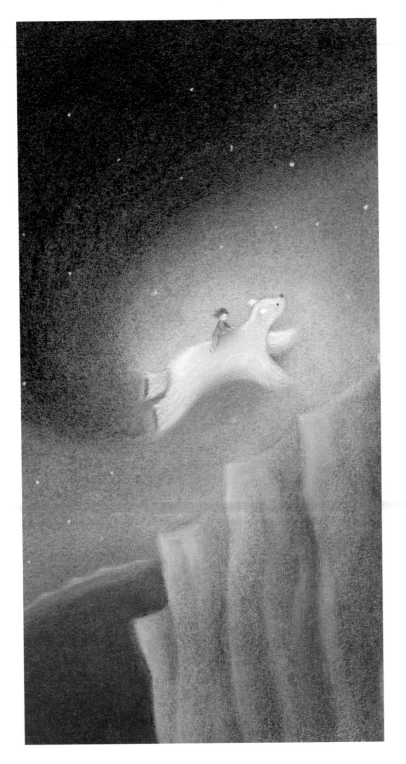

"Over the cliffs,

as sharp as giants' teeth . . .

past a great forest
that shook like shaggy bears . . .

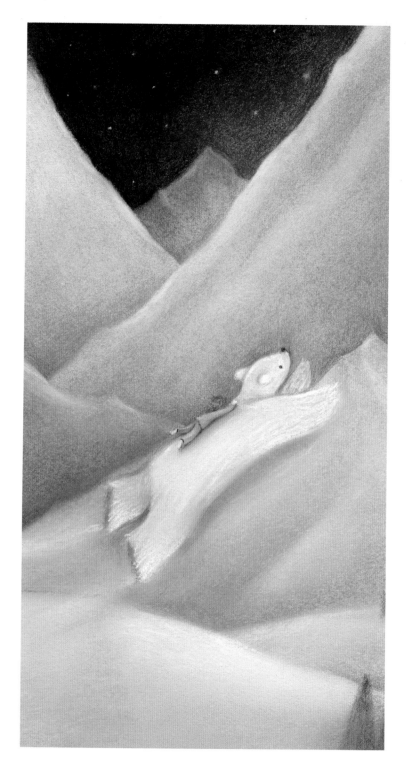

to the top of a glittering mountain of ice.
The wind howled like a hundred wolves!"

"That sounds scary,"
said Dad . . .

21

"Not if you're a polar bear!" said Jamie.
"We were the kings of the mountain. It was dark and sparkly and beautiful!"

"And then you were sleepy," Dad said.
"A little . . ." Jamie yawned.

23

"So the wind blew you home," said Dad. "It whirled and swirled and dropped you gently in the yard, like two tired leaves."

"It was dark as you
crept up the stairs to bed.
But Polar Bear wasn't scared.
**Because polar bears
aren't scared of anything."**

25

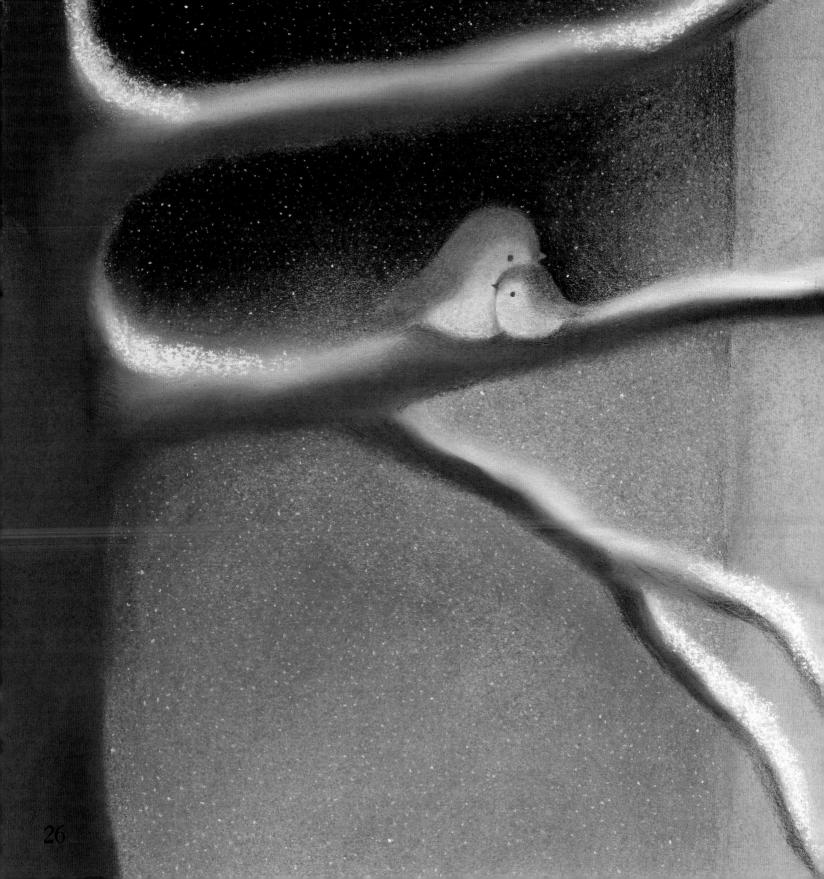

"Neither are polar bear boys," murmured Jamie.

"Goodnight, Polar Bear Boy," whispered Dad.

27

Little Rabbit
Waits for the Moon

Little Rabbit
couldn't sleep . . .

29

In the day,
the sun is there, warm
and bright. But when night comes,
the sky hangs low, dark, and empty.

30

"If I fall asleep now, there'll be no one watching over me," thought Little Rabbit. "I'll just have to wait for the moon." And so he did just that.

31

The trouble with being so tired and sleepy,
was that he didn't know exactly when
the moon would come.

Little Rabbit waited and waited.

More time passed and the moon still
hadn't come.

He thought he had better ask someone
how much longer he might have to wait.

"This is my first day, ever,"
said a small flower in the fields.
"Maybe I will have grown into a tree
by the time your moon comes."

That sounded like a very long time.

Little Rabbit thought he had better ask
someone else—just to be sure.

35

"Look deep into the water," shimmered a little lake nearby. "Maybe your moon has fallen in and can't get out."

That didn't sound like what he wanted to hear.

Little Rabbit thought he had better ask someone else—just to be sure.

"Why don't you walk with me?"
twisted a long and winding path.
"We can find out where I'm leading
and maybe your moon is at the
other end!"

That sounded like it might
be a long way away.

Little Rabbit thought he had better ask
someone else—just to be sure.

39

"I've just blown in to these parts," breezed a wind that had picked up. "Who knows? I might be a big, fierce storm by the time your moon comes."

That didn't sound like something he wanted to wait for.

Little Rabbit thought he had better ask someone else—just to be sure.

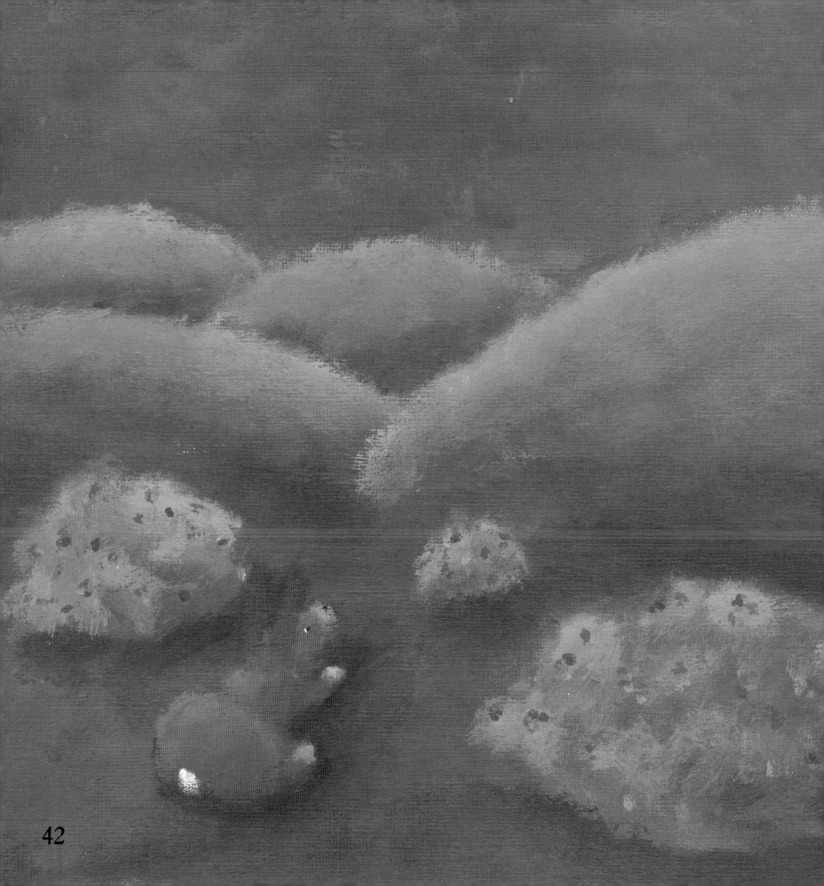

42

"We can't see your moon yet,"
rumbled the great, rolling hills.
"And we can see far into
the distance from up here!"

That didn't sound very promising.

Little Rabbit began to think that the
moon might never come. And he was
getting very, very tired . . .

And then, from behind the hills,
carried by the wind along the twists
of the path, reflected in the lake, and shining
on the petals of the small flower . . .

44

. . . the most perfect moon
slid into the night sky.

45

But Little Rabbit

had fallen asleep, dreaming

of the moon that would

watch over him through the night.

47

If Big can ...
I can.

If Big can run ...
    ... then I can run!

(Though not as fast,
I'm only small.)

If Big can jump …
   … then I can jump.

(And Big leaps long,
long, long away.)

If Big can swing …
… then I can swing.

(As Big swings
high into the sky,
I'll get there, too,
one day, I'm sure.)

53

If Big can climb ...
... then I can climb.

(It's just I have to take
my time to get to all the
places Big can climb to
with one stretch.)

55

If Big can see …
… then I can saw.

56

(Up, up I go, into the air.
I never thought I'd get so high,
but now that Big is on the ground,
how will I get down?)

If Big can play ...

... then I can play.

(Deep in the sand Big digs a hole ...

... but if I fell in I'd be stuck, and then I'd have to yell and shout for Big to come and pull me out!)

But what if Big
can't get into places
only I can squeeze inside?

I'd find the treasures,

rule the roost!

Be number one ...

And Big would know
I'm having fun.

If Big could only see ...

… how great it is
inside my den and all
the games I like to play
on oceans around the world
and spaceships in the sky.

Here I can swing into the air!

Running fast and leaping long

66

and stretching to climb
and soaring high
into the air
and digging deep ...

... but Big's not there ...

67

… I'm all alone …

… and that's no fun,

so …

Whatever Big can …

and whatever I can ...

We can …

72

... together!

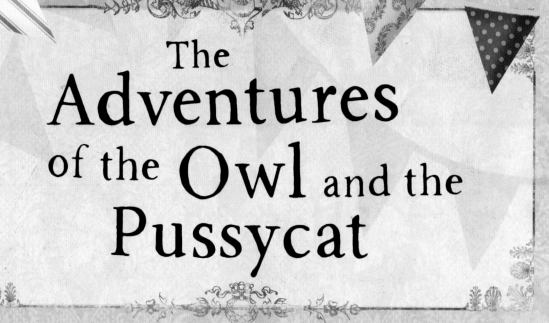

The
Adventures
of the Owl and the
Pussycat

The Owl and the Pussycat went to sea
In a box on the living room floor,
They sailed away for a year and a day,
And these are the things
that they saw ...

75

A wiggly, squiggly eel
Dancing with a cheerful seal,

A bottle bobbing by
With a treasure map inside,

A shark in a spin
With a cat on his fin,

79

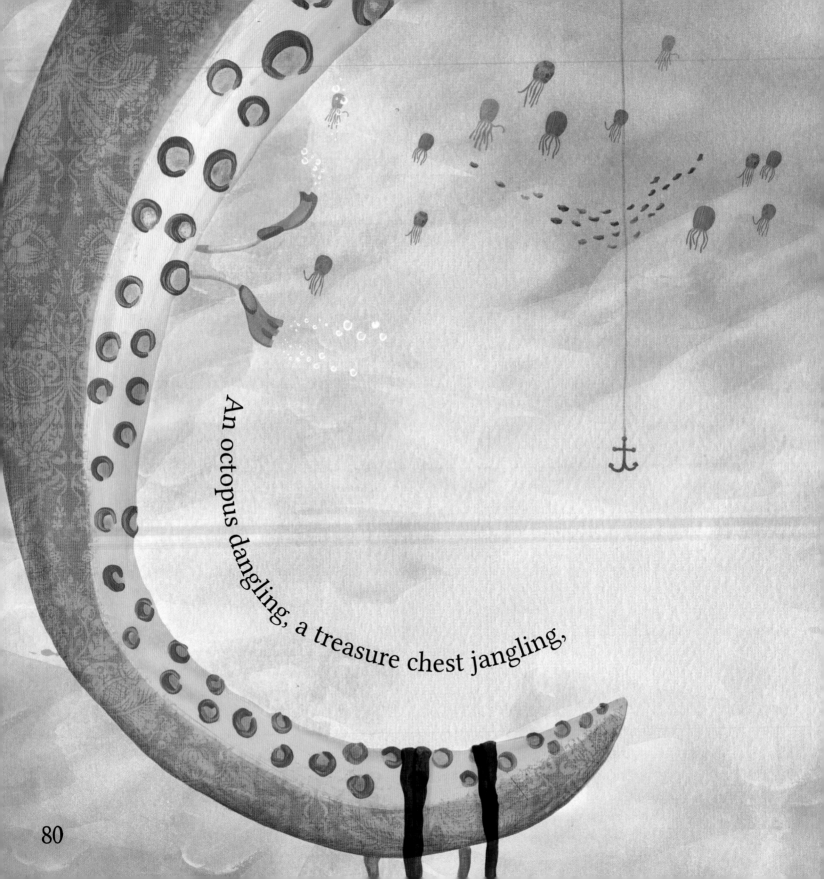

An octopus dangling, a treasure chest jangling,

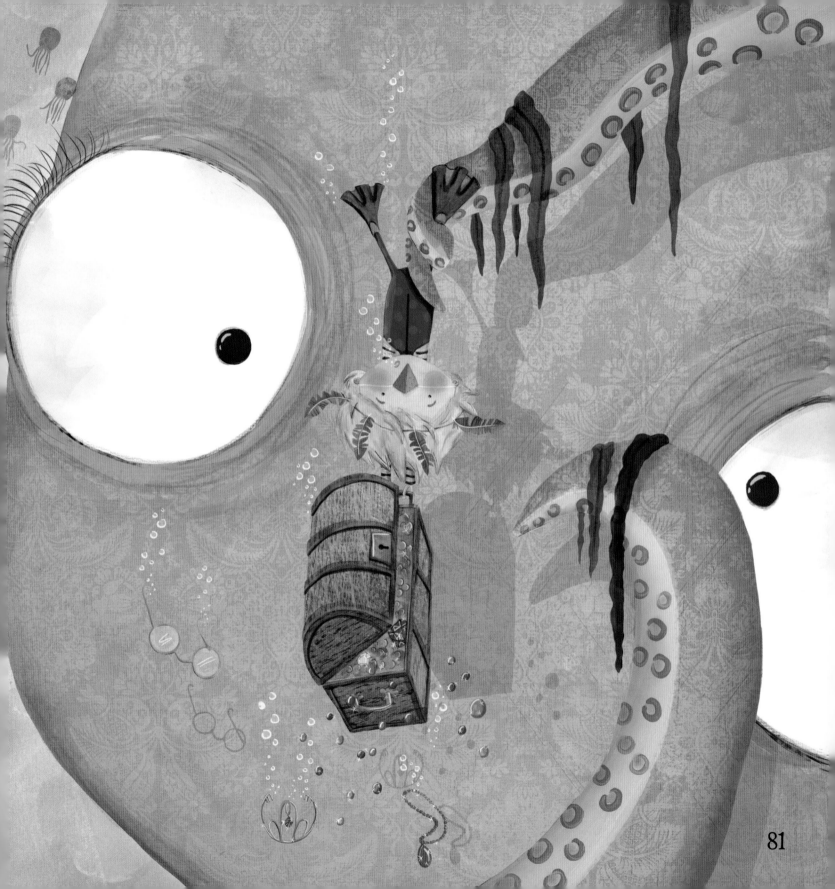

A clownfish playing the flute

In a bow tie and a suit,

83

A starfish in the sun,

84

A naughty seagull
having fun,

A lobster playing catch

86

With a crab who likes to snatch,

87

A swordfish in a fight
With a pirate late at night,

89

A puffin in a cap flying around the moon and back,

ARRRR LNJC *PIRATE COVE WELCOMES YARRRR*

7. 3. 2011

10.03.1987

CLASS OF 1980

04.06.82

WORLD CLASS FLYER 1982

Octupus' Garden

27 AUGUST 2005

ARRIVED: 20 SEPTEMBER 2005

WORLD TRAVELLER

Gold Star Traveller

06.26.1998

12.12.2012

FIRST CLASS

CLASS OF 2011 First Star Traveller

SWETHOD CLASS TUNNELL

04.26.11

10.20.1990

PUFFIN PASSPORT

Surname/Nom (1)
PUFFIN
Given Names/Prénoms (2)
AMELIA BELLE
Nationality/Nationalité (3)
ATLANTIC PUFFIN (F. AR
Date of birth/Date de naissance (4)
7 OCT / OCT 11
Sex/Sexe (5)
Place of birth/Lieu de
ICELAND

P<AVIANPUFFIN<<AMELIA<BELLE<
<<012368PUF02460>>>35798642

AB

THE BARRACUDA SCUBA JAZZ CLUB * THE BARRACUDA SCUBA JAZZ CLUB

SEAL DIVING CENTER

90
03. 03. 2008

OCTOBER

WELCOME TO
SHARK ISL
MIND YOU

14 DECE

A cave on the shore
With a green seaweed door ...

The Owl and the Pussycat went to sea
In a box without very much room.
Then, hand in hand, they sailed back to land
And slept by the light of the moon,
    the moon, the moon ...

And slept by the light of the moon.

95

If You Can ... We Can!

I love you …

I really do!

(Although my arms are just too small
and so I can't quite cuddle you.)

I hug you ...
you hug me.

(And around
and around
we dance together,
holding tight.

Don't let me fall!)

I make you laugh ...
   you laugh with me.
         (There's nothing in this world
            that can make us feel so good
               as laughter can, as laughter does,
               as laughter should.)

I hold your hand ...

you hold mine tight.

(Just feeling snug, secure, and safe.
Just knowing you'll protect me,
care for me ...
be there.)

I sing you songs …
    you sing them, too.

(Loud ones, soft ones,
    make-me-laugh ones.
Love songs, sleep songs,
    safe-and-sound songs.)

I tell you tales …
you listen close.

(Then tell me stories
through the night …

of mighty dragons,
gallant knights …

adventures made
to fill my mind.)

I'm in your dreams ...
and you're
in mine.

(The best dreams, safe dreams,
sleep-all-night dreams.
My dreams, your dreams.
Always our dreams.)

Let's be friends forever, I say!

There for one another,
looking out and taking care.

So ...

112

Whatever you do ...

114

and whatever I do ...

Let's do it …

... together!

HERNANDO FANDANGO
The Great Dancing Dog!

He's clever, **adventurous**, courageous, and mighty,
(And ever so handy for storing a nightie),
HERNANDO
FANDANGO, pajama-case dog,
Is the very best friend of Miss Adelaide Mogg.

119

Now, of all the fun things they did together,
Dancing gave them the greatest pleasure!

In Adelaide's room, they would
     practice each day ...

JAZZ,

Ballroom
dancing,

Tap,

and

Ballet!

Secretly dreaming of a shiny dance floor,
With a crowd of fans cheering

"ENCORE! ENCORE!"

And, as it happened, by the most amazing of chances …

121

Adelaide's parents were REAL ballroom dancers!

The foxtrot, the rumba,
    the American smooth,
The quick step, the samba—
    they knew every move!

Hernando and Adelaide never grew tired,
Of watching them dance—they felt so inspired!

Now Adelaide's parents were preparing to be
Part of a dance show, to compete on TV!

The big day was near,

so they shimmied

and hopped,

They twirled and whirled

and danced ...

till they **dropped!**

125

The competition day duly arrived,
The dancing began, they waltzed, then they jived.

126

The Moggs looked so graceful, they'd practiced so much,
Surely nothing could come between them and the cup!
But ...

127

With the cameras rolling
and MILLIONS tuned in,
To see all the couples
doing their thing ...

Two couples collided ...

128

a dancer's **worst** fear,

A pair of **sprained** ankles—the Moggs couldn't appear!

The host shouted out,

"Do we have
any dancers?"

Adelaide knew this was
the rarest of chances.

She longed to cry out,
But she wasn't that brave,

And already a figure
had taken the stage!

Can you guess who it was,
who could waltz, jive, and tango ...?

131

Of course—it was ...

HERNANDO FANDANGO!

Courageous and mighty,
pajama-case dog,
Reached for the hand
of Miss Adelaide Mogg.

132

She smiled at Hernando
and, taking his paw,
Took a deep breath
and stepped onto the floor!

So, they started to waltz, Miss Mogg and her hound,
And, as they danced, the best friends found
That their dream had come true!
They swished round the floor,

The music was playing!
The crowd gave a ROAR!

135

Their waltz
was **divine**,

and so was
their **shuffle**,

Their cha-cha-cha
caused quite a **kerfuffle!**

And, lo and behold,
for the next **big band** number,
Hernando and Adelaide
were **dancing** the **rumba!**

136

Now for the voting, from across the nation!
Who would be the new **dance sensation?**

(Long pause
for effect ...)

"Ladies and gentlemen,
the winners are ..."

"Adelaide Mogg and

HERNANDO FANDANGO,

the Great Dancing Dog!"

Everyone **cheered**, the nation was right, Hernando and Adelaide were the **stars** of the night.

So Adelaide and Hernando held hands—and paws—And they took their bow to **rapturous** applause.

138

He's clever, adventurous, courageous, and **mighty**,
(And ever so handy for storing a nightie),

Hernando Fandango, pajama-case dog,
Is the very **best friend** of Miss Adelaide Mogg.

I Love You,
Alfie Cub

Alfie Cub bounced through the den.
"It's the morning!" He was ready to play.

"Look," said his mother.
"I have a surprise for you . . ."

141

"Two new twin sisters!"

Alfie's sisters were tiny and fast asleep.
"When will they be big enough to play with?" he asked.
"They'll grow fast," said his mother, "just like you did.
They need lots of food and lots of sleep,
and lots and lots of love."

Alfie watched
and waited all day.

His mother
fed the twins.

She kept them
warm while they slept
**and gave them
lots and lots
of love.**

"They aren't any bigger,"
said Alfie at bedtime.
"Not yet." His mother smiled.
"But they've kept me busy.
Night-night." She yawned
and nuzzled him close.
"I love you, Alfie Cub."

Next morning, the twins were *still* little.

"I'm afraid you'll have to play by yourself today,"
sighed Alfie's mother. "Two tiny cubs are a lot of work."

Alfie chased his tail.
He climbed a fallen tree. He followed
a butterfly through the woods.

But it wasn't much fun
on his own.

147

At bedtime, Alfie's mother was too tired to tell him a story.
"Night-night," she said, and with a yawn, fell fast asleep.

She didn't say "I love you," thought Alfie,
and his eyes prickled with tears.
"She must have run out of love."

149

But the next morning, Alfie had an idea.
"If Mommy has run out of love," he said,
"I will find her some more!"
So he tiptoed out of the den to look.

Alfie searched **high**

and low.

151

He searched **inside** and **out**,

over and **under**.

He found a big **pinecone**, a beautiful **flower**, and a bright **feather** . . .

But he didn't find any love.

A big, fat teardrop rolled off of Alfie's nose
and splashed into the stream.

153

Up popped Frog.
"Hello, Alfie! Why are you looking so sad?"
"I need some love for my mommy," said Alfie.
"She's given it all away."

"Hmm," said Frog, thoughtfully.
"Well, *you* haven't run out of love, have you?"
"No," said Alfie.

"So why not give her some of yours?"

"Of course!" said Alfie. "Thank you, Frog!" Away he ran, all the way home . . .

155

... and gave his mother
the tightest, squeeziest,
fox cub hug!

Alfie's mother held him close
and tickled his ears with kisses.
"I love you,
Alfie Cub!"
she said.

Alfie gasped.
"I thought you had run out of love!"
"Oh, I will never run out of love,"
said his mother. "Maybe your sisters
have just kept me too busy to show it."

That gave Alfie an idea . . .

157

He hung up pinecones and feathers,
and made them spin and rattle and roll.
The very little cubs watched happily,
all afternoon until bedtime.

"What an excellent
big brother you are,"
Alfie's mother said proudly . . .

159

But Alfie didn't answer. All the fun had worn him out!

"Night-night, Alfie Cub," whispered his mother.
"I will never, ever run out of love for you."